MARRYING THE WIDOWED DOCTOR

IRIS WEST

To you, my reader. I hope you love Blossom Ford, and the sexy men, curvy women and kind but extremely interfering folk that live there, as much as I do.

CHAPTER ONE

Liam

I USED TO think middle age crisis was an excuse to do crazy things. However, I'm starting to believe it is a thing. Nothing else, rational that is, can explain the fact that I'm considering marrying a woman matched to me by a matchmaking agency, only a few days after my forty-first birthday. Especially when the woman I loved and built a family with has only been gone three and a half years.

My hands tighten around a smiling picture of Lucy, taken before our marriage, her auburn hair flying and once again the certainty that I have to follow through with this marriage, however crazy it is, solidifies in me. I have to keep the promise she forced me to make on our wedding night; I would find someone to love and be a mom for our children if anything happened to her.

Loving is out of the question. Never again do I want to go through the agonizing pain of losing a woman I love. Besides, even if it's possible to fall in love again, how can I live with the kind of happiness I shared with Lucy when she's not here?

I can, however, fulfill the mom part.

"Daddy, Ollie is pulling my hair." Olivia hides behind me as her twin brother chases her.

I place the picture on a shelf and pick up my four-year-olds, one on each arm. They give me the strength to keep the silly promise I made.
I first started thinking about marriage when the twins were three and turned into monsters. Their nanny fell pregnant and quit to be a full-time mum.

None of the nannies that came afterwards could control them or deal with the uncertainty of the long hours I worked, when urgent surgeries became necessary. Then a couple of weeks ago, during Christmas dinner at Lucy's parents in New York, Olivia declared Santa was bad because he hadn't provided the first present on her list–a mom.

I want to do everything I can to make Liv and Ollie happy. That's what I'll focus on. It's the only way to make sense of me going ahead with an arranged marriage.

The bell rings.

"Be nice to the lady and each other." I place the kids on the floor beside a pile of toys. Squaring my shoulders, I march to the door and open it.

The smile of welcome freezes on my face. My breath hitches. Large sea-green eyes set in an oval-shaped face with the most kissable lips I've ever seen stare up at me for what seems like ages before I realize I'm staring back. The picture the agency sent didn't do justice to the curvy woman standing in the cold. The honey of her cheeks and the black of her long coat give the snow-covered garden color.

"Miss. Clark?"

She nods.

I move aside to let her pass, then take her coat. In tight-fitting black jeans and a red blouse that complements smooth honeyed skin, her curves are even more alluring. So is the scent of roses coming from her. My cock stirs.

Calm down and breathe.

I hung up the coat, and stride to the sitting room, annoyed at my reaction. It's unwanted and improper. In the last three and a half years, I've come across many attractive women, yet I never showed the slightest interest. Why now when I'm about to check whether Angel Clark would make an excellent mother for my kids?

The moment she spots the twins, she heads straight for them, sits cross-legged on the floor near them and says hi.

They watch her. A couple of minutes pass. Ollie traipses to her. Grabs her ponytail with his chubby hands and pulls. Angel reaches for him, tickles until he's giggling and releases her hair. He falls onto her lap, squirming.

"That's the consequence of pulling my hair. I won't stop tickling." There is laughter in Angel's face and her hands are gentle.

My lips tug up when Liv moves closer to the duo on the floor, hazel eyes identical to her brother's wide.

"Are you big sister Liv?" Angel asks.

Olivia nods.

"I'm Miss. Angel." She stretches out a hand.

Liv's eyes move from the hand to Ollie, who's still sitting on Angel's lap, then back to the hand. She shakes it.

Warmth spreads through my chest. Ollie and Liv fight like cats and dogs, but Liv is very protective of her brother. Although they are only a few minutes apart, he's developing at a much slower pace than her. Pleasing him is one way to get on her good side.

"He's Ollie." Liv sits in front of Angel, copies her cross-legged pose and studies her.

"I have to talk to Miss Angel, so come and draw," I say to the twins after they've had a little chat with Angel.

I settle Liv and Ollie in the kitchen with crayons and drawing pads. When I return to the sitting room, Angel is gazing at the photos spread all over the room of me and Lucy with the kids at different ages. In the most recent picture, the twins are six months old.

I sit and switch the monitor to listen to the kids, but

my eyes stray to Angel as soon as I'm done.

"I love Liv and Ollie," she says once she joins me in the sitting area.

That is something I like about her. How direct and decisive she is, despite being only twenty-four. I noticed it in her short profile statement and that, together with the fact she stated she's more interested in being a full-time mom rather than having a husband, is the reason I chose her. Her experience as a childcare provider is a bonus I'm grateful for.

"They like you. They rarely take to strangers. What do you think about the marriage now?"

A blush tints her cheeks, making me wonder what she's thinking. She turns away and studies a picture of the kids.

"I'll go ahead." She gazes at me, but I can't make the expression in her eyes.

"We have a deal, then."

Most of the paperwork for preparing the marriage, including a contract, was done online. She wanted to meet Liv and Ollie, and I had to see how the three of them interacted before making a final decision and signing the contract.

As the kids and I see Angel out, I remind myself why I'm marrying her–to get a mom for my kids. The reason I couldn't stop my eyes from watching the way her ass fit those tight jeans as she put her coat on was the three and a half years of celibacy my body endured. I may not be able to control the way I react to Angel, but that's okay, because my heart suffered so much after losing Lucy, it knows not to fall in love again.

CHAPTER TWO

Angel

I'VE DREAMED OF this day since I was a little girl; marrying a handsome groom I love and can rely on with my family and friends around me. Liam Johnson is the sexiest man I've ever seen and I'm already half in love with him and the way he cares for Liv and Ollie. The brilliant neurosurgeon will have no trouble providing for our family, too. But he doesn't love me.

Dad pats my hand. His sea-green eyes are steady as he looks at me. The butterflies in my tummy settle a little. As the wedding march song starts, I gaze at my flower girl and ring boy, Liv and Ollie, walking ahead of me. More butterflies settle. They are the reason I signed up for a marriage of convenience.

An accident when I was young left me unable to have kids. After my long-term boyfriend broke up with me because he realized he wanted to have his own kids rather than adopting, an arranged marriage became the only viable option I could think of.

When my eyes fix on Liam, I almost stop. He looks gorgeous in a tailored suit the color of his dark blue eyes. His shoulders are square, and he has that steady presence Dad always exudes. My nerves finally calm, but awareness of him as a man has my core clenching. Heat creeps up my neck towards my cheeks as I remember the hot dreams I've been having since I met him at his house just over a week ago. Taking in a long breath, I command myself to focus on the kids I already think of as mine and the friends and family in the registry office.

As soon as I reach the altar, all I can think about is Liam again. The moment his steady gaze fixes on me, I'm trapped. I try to concentrate on the words Mrs. Green, the officiant, is saying, as this is a special moment. I've been to a few friends and family weddings and always thought of the day my time would come.

"I take this woman to be my lawfully wedded wife from this day forward," Liam says in his deep voice when Mrs. Green prompts him.

My heart races. I don't think I'll ever forget these words or the way his voice sounded when he stated them, strong like he was promising himself I was his to care for, like he's pledging the words to his inner self.

A shiver runs through me. Mrs. Green clears her throat. I realize it's my time to say the vows. In the strongest voice I can manage, I say the words back to Liam.

His best man and colleague Jamal, also a widower, helps Ollie bring the ring to us. My eyes tear when the little boy stretches his hands out, his ivory, chubby cheeks puffed out with importance.

Liam takes my hand and slides the ring down my finger. His hands are firm; I can't help remembering what they were doing in my dream the night before. I'm not as steady as him when it's my turn to put the ring on him.

"You may kiss the bride," Mrs. Green's voice is filled with joy and anticipation.

Liam's eyes are a stormy blue as he gazes at me and slowly leans forward. I stand on my tiptoes. When his lips finally touch mine, they are soft and warm. Heat ignites in my core and I want a deeper touch. Liam pulls back. He watches me like he wants more. Then he blinks and that passionate stare is gone.

Mrs. Green congratulates us, and a teary Granny comes up and envelops me in her arms.

"Penny, you'll ruin her dress," Mrs. Green says.

"Now the wedding is done, the dress needs running." Granny wiggles her brows, making everyone laugh.

I'm sure I'm as red as a tomato now. I pick up Ollie

and ruffle his hair. Then my work mates surround me, and a little sadness fills me. I've worked at Smart Teddies Day care Center for six years. Since my high school friends left Blossom Ford to attend college and settled out of town, my work mates have become close friends. I'm going to miss them and the kids.

"Be happy Angel. Thank you for everything you've done for me and my little boy," Willow whispers when the others are congratulating Liam.

I hug her, glad that my new friend is looking so well. She was a bruised rag doll when she first came to Blossom Ford a year ago.

Mum calls out to everyone to pose for a picture and, of course, she wants photos outside, even though it's freezing, and everyone is complaining of the late January cold.

I'm sure Liam would've preferred foregoing all ceremonies, but he's smiling with Granny and Dad. Even when we have our first dance to a slow song in the marquee set up in our large backyard, he's a gentleman.

"You're a wonderful dancer," I say after he twirls me and catches my waist, neatly preventing a fall.

I watch his face light up, the crinkles around his eyes giving them a youthful look.

This is what he must have always looked like before his wife passed.

"You follow easily."

He twirls me again, and a thrill runs through me. By

the time the music stops, I'm not sure if I'm glad or sad. Isn't it dangerous for me to love his company too much?

But when he wipes a crumb of cake off the side of my mouth after feeding me a forkful, I know protecting my heart is going to be an uphill battle.

I feed him back to loud cheers. Then, I'm dragged onto the small dance floor by my friends for a lively song.

"Your family is lovely," Liam says when we have a moment to ourselves after he's danced with Mum, Granny and some of my friends.

"I guess it's hard for us to do quiet. You don't mind all the rituals, do you?"

"Liv and Ollie have been having fun." He looks to where the twins are playing with a small group of kids. "They're loving having another set of grandparents, too. I think they are going to be very spoiled. I haven't had this much fun in a long time."

It'd be easier to keep my heart intact if he weren't kind. I wanted a beautiful wedding like this, but my parents and Granny, who only have one child and grandchild, would have been heartbroken if they hadn't been able to have at least this small celebration when I married. If it had been up to them, everyone in town would have received an invitation and the reception would be at the best wedding venue in town.

The fact Liam is doing everything to make sure I have a memorable wedding tugs at my heartstrings and

I want him to be truly mine. However, he was clear from the beginning of our arrangement that he wasn't looking for love. A mother for his children, companionship, and a sexual partner were all he wanted. He'd made it clear his heart wasn't available.

CHAPTER THREE

Liam

IT'S PAST MIDNIGHT. I should be exhausted, yet all I can think about is the woman lying in bed with me, smelling of roses. It's a fragrance I'm growing very fond of and have begun to associate with Angel.

The kids were asleep when we arrived home. They didn't even wake up as we carried them into their bedroom and tucked them in bed.

Angel and I took turns using the bathroom. I thought she'd be tired, and suggested we sleep, even though the amount of skin her red camisole and shorts exposed made my dick stand to attention.

Her scent and knowing her honeyed skin and kissable lips are only an arm's length away, drove me straight to a raging hard-on. I've been breathing regularly for the past half-hour, trying to control myself, but every time I think I'm getting a handle on my body, she moves.

"Are you asleep?" Her voice is soft.

I turn to her. My eyes adjusted to the soft moonlight in the room long ago. I lie on my side, facing her.

"No. Are you tired?" I can't control the need in my voice.

She shakes her head.

"I can't stop thinking about touching you," I say.

I can't make out her expression. There isn't enough light.

"Me too." She lies on her side too. "We are married."

A laugh escapes me. I really like how pragmatic she is. I switch on the bedside lamp. Her lips are tugged up. With the tip of one finger, I trace them. She bites the finger and my cock jerks.

I close the distance between us and kiss her. Her arms snake around my head as she angles her head.

"I've wanted to do this since the moment I saw you," I whisper against her mouth when I come up for air.

"Don't stop then."

Laughter ripples through me until her nails scrape across my back. I remove my t-shirt. I want those nails on my skin.

She slips her camisole off too, freeing two large, rounded breasts with dusky, almost black nipples. They are so pretty; a little pre-cum spills off me.

I kiss each tip reverently. Then take one into my mouth and suck, pulling strongly.

"Yes, Liam."

"You like?" I rub my lips against the hard tip, take her other nipple into my mouth, licking it like candy before I suck on it.

A moan and another rake down my back are the answer.

I stroke up the sides of her chest, then slip my hand past the swell of her tummy. I grab her shorts and panties and pull them down her beautiful, thick legs, then quickly strip my sweatpants.

I want this night to be good for Angel. She's given up on having a husband who's in love with her, but there's no reason she can't have great sex.

"You're beautiful!" I'm not just saying it to please her. I'm so turned on by her curves, taking time to please her won't be easy.

"You too." She's looking at my cock like it's her favorite dessert.

I play with the soft curls on her mound, then pet her clit until she's undulating against my finger. Her nub is so hard, I want to taste it. I lick it twice, then take it into my mouth and suck hard. I slip two fingers into her wet pussy, then a third, and pump in and out of her.

"That's so good," she hums.

Her hands are tight around my neck, pulling me to her. Right now, there's no place I'd rather be. With a cry, Angel comes apart, convulsing against my mouth and hand. I slide up her body and kiss her, loving the way she looks right now, her sea-green eyes cloudy with pleasure and her face relaxed with satisfaction.

I place my aching cock against her folds and bury myself to the hilt in her, her juices and my pre-cum easing my penetration. Even so, she's so tight around me; I groan. The sensation of her firm hands stroking my ass drives more pleasure through me. I set a fast pace, a wave of relief filling me as Angel meets my every thrust.

She wraps her legs around me, allowing me to bury deeper into her with each thrust.

"Liam," Angel shouts against my neck.

I slip a hand between us and stroke her clit.

She contracts around my cock, her legs tightening around my ass, and I come violently, bucking as a stream of hot cum jets into her pussy. When I'm spent, it takes all my energy to roll over, so she's lying on top of me, and my dead weight is not pressing on her.

"Okay?"

Her upper body shakes against my chest. It takes me a few seconds to realize she's laughing.

"I'm much more than okay. I think I got myself a very skillful husband in the bedroom department."

My laugh comes from deep inside me. It's loud, unrestrained and surprises me a little. It's been a long time since I laughed like this.

"And I got myself a beautiful, sexy wife that drives me to distraction and is so responsive to my touch, I'm afraid I'll be spending way too much time thinking about night-time when I can her into bed."

As I fall asleep, a wash of gratitude for Angel comes over me. With her, I can have great sex and maybe friendship while Liv and Ollie get a terrific mom. Angel seems to already love them and enjoyed having sex with me. Our hearts are not at all involved. Already, our arranged marriage is getting off to an excellent start.

CHAPTER FOUR

Angel

I WAKE UP to muscular arms wrapped around me. Rays of sunshine slip through the curtains, illuminating the room. What we did last night flashes through my mind and a wave of pleasure ripples through me.

Large hands glide through my back and cup my butt cheeks, fondling them. I shiver again. It would be brilliant if I could wake up like this every day. I snake my hand past Liam's hard abdomen and circle his semi-hard cock.

"Good morning," I whisper. I turn my head so I'm looking at him. His eyes are closed. I slide my hand up and down his length.

"It's a delightful morning," his voice is strained.

Voices come from the monitor.

"Let's go wake Daddy and Mommy."

Rustling noises follow.

I release Liam. He pulls away from me. Red suffuses his cheeks. He looks cute and unlike his usual assured self; I chuckle.

"It's not funny. They'll be here any minute."

"If they ask, we can say we undressed because we were hot."

Liam helps me look for my clothes and finds my camisole and panties. We put our underwear on before Liv's voice sounds outside the door. Like naughty children, we jump under the covers. The door bursts open.

"Daddy, are you awake?" Liv calls out loudly.

Both children run to the bed and climb on.

"Didn't you sleep? You woke up too early," Liam says to the kids after we've greeted them.

They tuck themselves in between us, their eyes wide with interest.

"Silly Daddy. The sun is shining. It's morning," Liv says.

"I'm hungry," Ollie cries, rubbing his tummy.

Liam looks at me, black curls tousled, eyes full of resignation. As much as I want the pleasure I know he can dish out, I'm fascinated by the picture the four of us make.

"How about pancakes and eggs?" I ask the three of them.

The kids cheer and scramble over Liam in their rush

to get out of bed.

"I'm going to use the toilet first. I'll be there in a minute," I say.

Liam strolls out with them, holding a child in each arm. They say nothing about his navy boxers, but I stare at his butt until he catches me looking when he turns to close the door. I hide my face under the blankets, a little embarrassed by how much I want him.

I get out of bed, wash quickly, and slip on my favorite old jeans and a snug sweater. In the kitchen, Liv and Ollie are sitting at the table with small glasses of orange juice in front of them. Liam is rummaging through cupboards.

"I have all the ingredients here," he says.

When I'm within touching distance of him, he leans closer. "I'm going to wash and get dressed."

"What are you hiding, Daddy?" Ollie asks.

"Mommy and Daddy stuff," Liv's whisper is so loud I can hear it.

A silly grin spreads over my face, but I don't care. For a while, when I found out I couldn't have children, I didn't think I'd ever hear anyone call me mom. And that devastated me. I was only sixteen, but even though some of my friends couldn't understand my decision, I knew I wanted to be just like my mom and be a full-time mother and homemaker.

Liam ruffles the twins' hair as he leaves the kitchen, and my heart explodes with happiness. I'm in love with him. He's generous to me and respectful of my family.

I love how he's so affectionate to his kids and adores them, and I love his gorgeous body.

He's such a straight-forward person, that even though he can't give me his heart, as long as we can have a friendly relationship and love the kids together, I'll be happy. I'll just have to make sure he doesn't find out about my feelings. I don't want our relationship to be awkward when he was clear from the beginning love wasn't a part of our marriage.

Friends with benefits, that's what we'll be. I can do it.

I realize the kids are gazing at me.

"Who wants to make pancakes?"

I move the ingredients to the table so they can help and search through drawers until I find overalls, then help Liv and Ollie put them on.

Liam saunters back into the kitchen, also wearing a sweater and jeans, his hair wet and slicked back.

"I'm not sure about this." His eyes widen when Ollie grabs the bag of flour.

"If you join in, it'll be fun."

He rushes to his boy's side and helps him scoop out the flour.

"How much?" He asks Ollie, who looks at me.

"About half."

I'm helping Liv crack the eggs into a small bowl when a chortle and a muffled curse breaks my concentration. Ollie is giggling; his hands are white, and bits of flour are stuck to his head. He's pointing to his dad, who also has flour on parts of his body.

Liv joins in. I try not to, but Liam looks so struck I can't help it. I crack up. He takes a while to see the funny side of this spectacle, but soon, he's chuckling too.

CHAPTER FIVE

Liam

"CAN YOU CLOSE her up?" I ask my assistant neurosurgeon.

"Of course," Lori answers, a glint in her eye I know too well. We've been operating for twelve hours, yet she wouldn't dream of saying no, even if she had a choice. She's one of the best fellows that's ever worked under me and reminds me of myself in the way she's married to her patients and spends so much time at the hospital, it's no wonder the twins' nannies couldn't handle the unpredictability of my hours and quit often.

Before we had the twins, Lucy was so engrossed in her art sometimes I'd get home after being away most of the day and she'd be surprised when I arrived, completely unaware of the passage of time. It was frustrating, but the way she could focus on a particular task for so long was one of the things that fascinated me about her. After the babies were born, our nanny was always around, still I sometimes wonder if Lucy wanted me home more often.

"The operation was successful. We excised the tumor. Have a well-deserved rest, so you can care for your wife when she's awake," I say to my patient's husband.

I stretch my arms and circle my shoulders and neck as I head to my office. There's an excellent coffee machine there, a present Lucy gifted me when we moved to Blossom Ford five years ago, however I'm too tired to wait and grab an expresso from a vending machine. I quickly take care of paperwork and leave the hospital by nine.

Outside Weston-Parker General, I head east towards home to a part of town under the mountains of Blossom Ford. Lucy fell in love with the area and although the house she wanted required lengthy renovations, she insisted we buy it. We lived on the other side of town, near Blossom Ford Point for the year it took to renovate and decorate the house the way she wanted to.

It's still hard how she passed six months after Liv and Ollie were born, from a car accident, only days before our move in date. I blink and blink again. Every day, things like a scent or painting remind me of her, but today, it was the worry on the face of my patient's husband, his fear that he'd lose her.

It takes fifteen minutes to get home from the hospital and soon I'm pulling into the driveway. Anticipation runs through me when I think of Angel waiting for me inside and having a meal with her. She's on her knees in the sitting room, peering behind the sofa. My eyes lock on the way her ass fills out the soft pants she's wearing and just like that, I want her. That's all it takes, a look, touch, or the sound of her voice.

"Got you!" She waves a soft toy in the air, spots me mid-celebration and smiles.

I march over, and pull her against me, the scent of roses and the feel of her soft body against mine so familiar, I'm thinking of moments like this at the end of a long day as home, even though we've only been married three weeks.

"Tough day?"

"Complex operation. The patient's tumor was large and in a difficult position. A tiny slip could have meant paralysis. The chances of survival weren't high either."

"I guess they were lucky they got the best neurosurgeon in the world."

Laughter bubbles out of me.

"That's what everyone says. I'm not being biased."

"Your Gran?"

"She knows everything that happens in Blossom Ford. Apparently, some nurses and female doctors are disappointed they missed out on marrying you. Now, get in the shower while I warm dinner. If we stay like this any longer, you might miss it again and Granny will start saying I'm not feeding you."

I laugh again as Angel extricates herself from our embrace and rushes to the kitchen, as if she's tempted to stay.

The twins are sleeping soundly when I open the door to the nursery, Liv on her tummy in her favorite pajamas and Ollie cuddling his toy. I shower quickly, eager to try out whatever Angel made today.

"This is amazing," I say after a bite of chili con carne and tuck into the rest of the food. "You can open a restaurant with skills like these." She told me she'd learned to cook from her gran and Mom.

"I love cooking! Caring for kids is my favorite thing to do though."

"How did you know you wanted to be a homemaker? And a childcare worker?"

She finishes her bite of food and sips wine. "Mom is the best in the world. I don't know if it's because she had me late in her life, but she cooked and baked with me, made sandcastles and dolls' clothing. Even though Dad was busy at work, on weekends we rode our bikes to Blossom Ford Point, watched movies, and hang out with Granny. I was loved so much, I wanted to give back to other children. I wanted to be like Mom."

There's a sparkle in Angel's eyes and an energy around her that makes me want to hear her talk.

"My parents divorced when I was six. I had a couple of stepfathers, but they were busy living their own lives.

I assume Mom and Dad did things with me before things soured between them; I don't remember. Going fishing and to the ball game with your dad is the first fatherly outing I remember. It's good to hear him call me son, too. And my colleagues love the scarves your mom makes for me."

"You know he's going to keep pestering you to support the local team, right? And just wait until Mom knits you jumpers."

The look of horror on her face is so comical; my lips lift.

"The ones she made Liv and Ollie are beautiful."

"They are cute on kids. Now imagine a bright yellow sweater with green and purple leaves on the front."

"I get it. Doesn't she make them for you? All your sweaters are beautiful."

Her face turns pink. I never thought I was the type that was attracted by a woman blushing, yet I get a kick out of seeing Angel's reaction whenever I compliment her.

"I have a couple of friends who love Mom's sweaters and live out of town. They steal them off me."

"You send it to them knowing they'll love them." I like the mix of sweetness and cheekiness in her personality.

"I've never heard you talk about your parents before."

"We're not very close. Mom is on her fourth husband. I believe Dad is on his fifth. I had nannies until I was about twelve. After I left for college, I only saw them twice. We exchange Christmas cards. That works for us."

Angel's eyes soften. She places her hand on mine, where it lies on the flowery tablecloth. "My parents will be yours, too. And if you ever want to get closer to yours, we can always visit them. Maybe they want to spend more time with you, but it's been so long, they feel awkward about it."

My heart stutters.

I'm in love with this woman.

CHAPTER SIX

Angel

A WEEK LATER, I'm having lunch with Willow at Jackson's Diner. Mom gets to spoil our kids rotten whilst I get a break from the twins and Willow enjoys her day off without a kid in tow.

"There's something about diner fries I love. I've been trying to cook healthy meals at home; it's nice to have this treat," I say, anticipation filling me as I stare at my loaded plate of cheeseburger and fries.

"I'd like to know what they put in this sauce. It'd sell fast, if it's bottled up."

I tuck into my food. "Old Jackson won't say. He's convinced someone will steal it from him. There's something different about you. Is it a man?"

Willow chokes on iced coke. I stretch across the small table and pat her back. Once the coughing fit passes, she shakes her head.

"Raising my little boy well is all that matters to me. He hasn't had a good start in life. I'm going to make sure he's happy."

For a moment she looks like she's about to say more, however her expression closes. That look is familiar. She won't say anything about her past, no matter how I press.

"Blossom Ford's Matchmaking Agency has a one hundred percent success rate, if you ever want to try marriage, so Jaiden can have a dad. And you never know, you and your matched husband might fall in love. Granny says the Navajo blood of the women who run the agency has foreseeing abilities and that's why every couple they match always ends up falling in love." It seems I'm the only exception.

"Just like you? You're in love with your husband. I see it in the way you watch and talk about him. You get this look when you're thinking about him, too."

It's my turn to splutter.

"Am I that transparent? I thought it was only my family that saw it."

"Sorry," Willow says. "Something is wrong, though. You're not your usual self."

I wish I'd had more success when I tried to learn how to hide my feelings. Does Liam know I'm in love with him, too? I hope not. Yet, I can't get rid of the niggling suspicion that he's noticing my feelings for him. What else can explain the way he's become distant from me?

It started the night he came home late from work and opened up about his parents. For the first time since our wedding, we didn't make love. It's been a week since then and he still hasn't touched me. Every time I tried to get closer, he'd say he was tired. He's coming home later too and spends more time in his study, the only place in the house I'm not welcome in. Where I suspect he spends time with the woman in his heart.

The twins have pictures of their mom in their bedroom, but the other rooms in the house have pictures of the four of us. I'm sure the study has pictures of the first Mrs. Johnson. That's why Liam told me he'd clean the room himself.

"It's nothing, really. I love being a mom and Liam is generous. He offered to get me help." I'm not ready to share what's happening with Liam.

"I bet that's not all he's generous with." She wiggles her thick brows.

"How does your mind go there? Honestly, Willow." I hide my face by taking a long sip of my drink.

"I don't think it's the sex. Whatever it is, I hope you guys sort it out. You're so right for each other. Maybe it's true that agency can really foresee the future of couples."

Liam and I are right for each other. If he only opened up his heart and gave us a chance, he might fall in love with me. The way we are so explosive in bed leaves no doubt he's attracted to me. He likes me too. I see it in the way he ensures I'm always comfortable and genuinely listens to me raving on about mom programs.

Of course, I knew his heart wouldn't be mine from the beginning. I'd accepted friendship and brilliant sex together with the joy of seeing the kids grow as a family was as much as I was going to get from him.

But now even our friendship is at risk, and I don't know what I did to cause him to distance himself from me.

Sure, I miss the heat of his touch. However, I miss our chats and the way he holds me in his arms even more.

***

Liam

I FORCE MYSELF to eat the baked potato in the cafeteria, frustration at how much I've allowed Angel to become a part of my life filling me. I endured the food at work for years. It took Angel's food four weeks to spoil me to the point where I compare the taste of everything I eat with her cooking.

She got into the habit of packing sandwiches for me, but Liv has had a fever for the past couple of days and Angel has been taking care of her nonstop. She usually wakes up when I leave for work yet didn't stir this morning.

Before I left for work, I watched her sleep, the longing to wrap her in my arms so strong, I had to drag myself to work.

"Poor potato," Jamal says as he pulls a chair opposite me and sits down, tucking into his own potato. He rotates his neck and shoulders.

I look at my plate. The potato is now an untidy pile of mash.

"Extensive surgery?" I ask, giving up on the food.

"Emergency patient. I came in at three in the morning. I have another surgery after lunch. There isn't much point going home. Besides, there's a new nurse in general surgery. She's pretty. Maybe she's the woman I'm meant to be with. I'm having coffee with her in a little while."

I stare at him. "You were in love with Roshelle. I didn't think you'd ever laugh again without her in your life. Falling in love a second time might cause you pain, again."

Jamal watches me, a somber look in his eyes. "I can only hope it doesn't. Even if it does, I'd rather be with someone for the months, years we have than live without love. It isn't easy to find that special person meant for you. It's even harder to find a second special person."

He gulps half a bottle of water. "You found yours. If it happens to me, I'm not letting go, no matter how afraid I'll be to lose her again. If that's what's bothering you, I get it. I think I'd be the same. Just don't let that fear ruin your relationship. The way your eyes followed Angel on your wedding day, man, I hope I get to experience that again."

Was I that besotted even then?

I liked Angel from the beginning, but I didn't think it was possible for me to fall so deeply in love with another woman other than Lucy. Now I know what I feel for Angel is love. She's the first thing I think about when I wake up. I want to hear her talk about the mom programs she loves so much. I'm dying with need for her.

"Won't you feel guilty?"

"About being happy without her?" Jamal asks so quietly, it's hard to hear him in the jumbled chatter of the busy cafeteria. "Don't know. Guess I will, when the sorrow of her going so young hits me. But that happens less and less. More and more, I remember the good times. She'd want me to be happy again. Lucy would want the same for you. If the situation were reversed, you'd never expect her to remain single."

We walk silently around the hospital until my afternoon clinic starts and it's time for Jamal to meet the new nurse.

In between patients, I can't stop wondering about what Jamal said. I've been thinking less and less about Lucy, even before meeting Angel. I suppose this made me feel a little guilty. Falling in love again intensified that guilt. Also, I've always vowed I wouldn't be like Mom and Dad. When I met Lucy, I didn't believe in marriage. We dated for years before I mustered up the courage to trust our marriage would last. I swore to myself I'd always be loyal to her.

It's true I'd want Lucy to find another love. Why am I not giving myself the same chance? And I was loyal to Lucy for the rest of her life.

Half-way through the afternoon, I check up on Angel. Relief floods me when I realize her tired voice is back to normal. The way her eyes cloud up when I avoid spending time with her has been killing me. I can't bear the desolation in those pretty eyes anymore. She deserves better. Somehow, I'll have to deal with the fear of being in pain if anything ever happens to her.

CHAPTER SEVEN

Angel

I FROWN AS I spot Liam's car in the drive. It's only three o'clock. Officially, he finishes at six, even though lately he's been getting home close to ten or eleven.

Didn't he get my text that I'd be home?

While I was at Mom's, he called to say he'd forgotten a package was arriving today and wanted me home. We'd only just arrived, so Liv and Ollie refused to leave. Granny nearly pushed me out the door, uncharacteristically angry because she felt I wasn't trusting my family enough with my step kids. Which was utter rubbish.

Determined to have it out with her as soon as I receive the package and return to Mom's, I open the door. Maybe whatever Liam ordered is important and he can't wait to see it. If that is the case, I'll go back to

Mom's while he waits for the delivery.

Although it's killing me, I'm trying to respect his wish to keep his heart for his first wife, but I don't know if I can survive losing our friendship. The tense atmosphere around the house isn't good for the kids either. We've both looked cheerful around them, but if whatever's going on carries on for much longer, they'll notice. Kids are good at spotting these things. If I'm alone with Liam, I'm afraid I'll ask what's wrong before he's had time to deal with whatever made him change.

Before I turn into the kitchen, a flash of red catches my attention. There are rose petals on the floor. And I stepped on them without noticing. They lead to the sitting room. Soft music is coming from there as well.

"Liam?"

There's no answer. The scent of roses strengthens as I near the sitting room, just as I realize two of my favorite types of candles line the entrance. When I enter the room, my hand flies to my mouth.

One of Mom's large, multicolored picnic blankets is laid out in front of the fireplace. On it are plates of sandwiches, fruit, Granny's famous pumpkin pie, champagne and a few other treats.

A noise makes me turn. Liam is standing at the door, with an enormous balloon saying be my valentine and a bouquet of my favorite flowers in his other hand.

"Valentine's day was days ago," I blurt. How can I be thinking about how good he looks in the white button-down shirt he's wearing?

His eyes hold mine prisoner as he moves towards me, as if he's afraid I'll bolt. All I can do is stare at him.

"I've been a moron for the last couple of weeks. That night, when I told you about my parents, I realized I'd fallen in love with you."

Already in a state at the thought of what this indoor picnic might mean, my heart goes into overdrive. I can't even speak.

"I don't." He stops, breathes in. "I don't want to hide anything from you. I was scared shitless of falling in love again and facing the possibility of loss. And I felt guilty towards Lucy. I'm sorry it's taken me a while to sort my feelings out and be the man you deserve."

A tear rolls down my cheek. "Liam," it's all I can say. My throat is crammed with cotton wool.

"I know love isn't part of our contract. If you want to keep it that way, I'll do everything I can to hide the way I feel about you and be happy with being friends and co-parents. Just let me hope one day your caring and attraction for me might turn into love."

I jump into his arms, not caring where the flowers and balloon fall when he catches me. I hold his dear face in my arms and kiss him, exhilarating at the familiar touch of his tongue against mine. It's as if I've come home.

"I love you," I say when I come up for breath.

I smile at the wonder on his face.

"Since when?"

"When the agency sent me your photo, I figured I

was going to have trouble not falling for you. The day after our wedding, I knew I was head over heels for you."

"God, I love you Angel." He nibbles on my lips. "I guess I should be romantic and make sure we have the picnic first."

He's now sucking on the pulse at my neck. He must have felt how fast it was beating.

"This is more romantic," I say before he devours my mouth.

He shuffles to the sofa without our mouths breaking contact, which is difficult when he's trying to avoid the picnic.

We strip before falling on the large sofa.

"I want you in my mouth. You've given me so much pleasure that way. I've only done it a few times."

"Woman, you're going to kill me. I'm aching for you."

He flips me so my pussy is hanging over his mouth and I'm facing his hard cock. I shiver when I see liquid seeping from the opening at the crown. I wasn't comfortable doing this with my exboyfriend, but the few times I did it with Liam, he told me how to please him and was so vocal about enjoying my touch; my confidence has grown. My mouth waters. I'm surprised by how much taking him into my mouth turns me on.

He licks down the entire length of my slit. It feels amazing. My eyes close.

I envelop him in my mouth, stroking up, and down,

my hands playing with his balls. He purrs, the vibration against my nub making me shiver again. When he takes my entire clit in his mouth and sucks softly while kneading my butt cheeks, I choke on his shaft and squeeze his balls hard.

Liam's cock falls out of my mouth as he flips me again. He places both my arms above me.

"I was enjoying that." I lick my lips.

His pupils are dilated and the blue in his eyes is as dark as I've ever seen them. He's close to the edge. It turns me on so much, tears sting my eyes. After the failure of my long-term relationship, I never thought I'd have something like this. No one can grow up in a family like mine without high self-esteem, but knowing Liam adores my voluptuous curves and can carry me so easily adds another level to my excitement.

"If you carry on, you're going to finish me in seconds," he bites out, holding my arms down.

"What's wrong with that?"

He lets go and kisses my eyes, lips and nose. The touch is so tender, my arms wrap around him. My chest is tight.

"I want to make love to you slowly, with our arms around each other, this first time, which seems like it's the first time for the rest of our times together."

He enters me languidly, breathing hard. I tangle my ankles with his legs, caressing them with my feet. His strokes are lazy and so is the glide of his tongue against mine.

I rake my hands up and down his back, enjoying the feel of his skin and the sense of being owned body and soul.

"My very own angel," Liam whispers against my neck, his lips pulling on the erogenous spot there.

"Yes, I'm yours." I cry against him.

By the time Liam increases the pace and rams into me, I'm a bundle of nerves. The moment he touches my clit, I come, his name a wordless cry.

"Angel!" His cry is loud as his cum shoots up my womb.

"The package," I whisper tiredly as Liam embraces me.

"There's no package. It was a ruse to get you here."

Granny's anger makes sense now. It was all pretense.

"Kids…"

"They are sleeping with your mom tonight."

My eyes shut in bliss.

EPILOGUE

Liam

Six years later

IT'S OUR SIXTH wedding anniversary, yet I never tire of gazing at Angel's soft honeyed face on my chest when I wake up. We got used to sleeping this way. Even on the occasional days I'm held up at the hospital and find her sleeping, we always end up this way when morning comes.

I'm not working today, and the twins are off school. They are trying to be quiet but are making such a racket; I wonder how Angel can sleep through it. She's still refusing to have help around the house and insists on driving the kids to their various clubs. Sometimes her mom, Granny and dad go with her. Although I walk our cocker spaniels Dolly and Rufus before work, they still take up a lot of her time. She insists on coming when I walk them after work. I suppose it's no wonder she's tired.

Three knocks sound on the door. It's Liv. She's so full of energy, she always goes overboard with everything she does.

Liv marches in, followed by the dogs, who are wagging their tails.

"Wow! Seriously?"

She turns away, and I laugh at the fake haughtiness on her shoulders.

"What is it?" Angel wakes and sits up just as the dogs bounce on the bed.

"Mom, I can't believe how you and Dad are still so lovey-dovey with each other. Ew!" She approaches the bed and lays a waterproof tablecloth on top of the cover. "Happy wedding anniversary," she sings to the accompaniments of the dogs' barking.

Ollie walks in wearing an overall, a large tray in his hands. He deposits it gently on the tablecloth and uncovers the plates.

"Happy anniversary, Mom and Dad," he says more quietly.

"This is lovely, sweethearts! It smells incredible too. Did you make the toast, Liv? It's browned just right," Angel says.

"See." Liv turns to Ollie. "Even Mom said so. It's perfect."

I stop myself from laughing at Ollie's raised eyebrow. I catch Angel's eye and know she's attempting the same thing. Our boy is so serious, that even though our doctor says he's growing well, I worry sometimes.

"What do you think, Dad?" Liv asks.

I look at Ollie. He shrugs. "It looks okay to me," I say, smiling at him.

Liv can't cook, no matter how much Angel teaches her. She has too much going in her brain to have the patience cooking requires. Her mind is full of information about stars, comics and the latest exploits into space.

Last year, when he was only nine, Ollie won the Blossom Ford Pumpkin Pie Contest. He was smart enough to do well at school if he applied himself, but his grades were average. He was happiest in Food Technology class. Not only had he memorized all the recipes his teacher and mom taught him; his cooking was to die for.

Liv and Ollie make themselves comfortable on the bed and we tuck into breakfast. It's become one of our traditions. Breakfast in bed on our wedding anniversary. This year was the first I didn't help the kids.

"Granny Jess sent a card," Olly states.

Angel was right about Mom. She'd wanted to spend more time together, but wasn't sure how. We'd never be as close as Angel's family. I feel closer to Angel's mom and dad, still we talk over the phone and see each other more. Dad is still gallivanting about the world, and I wish him well.

Every year, the kids spend a week of their summer break with Lucy's parents, so their biological mom is still a part of their lives. After we confessed our love for each other, Angel put a picture of the twins and Lucy in the sitting room, saying their mom would always be a part of our family.

"Happy anniversary, Hun," Angel says, her sea-green eyes sparkling.

"Happy anniversary, my angel."

I'm looking forward to spending the day alone with my very own angel when the kids go to their grandparents.

The End

MARRYING THE SCARRED SOLDIER

CURVY BRIDES OF BLOSSOM FORD #6

Willow

IF ANYONE HAD told me I'd willingly put myself in a relationship again, I'd have laughed my head off. But here I am, in a secluded wooden cabin in the woods, married and willing at that. Out of the corner of my eyes, I take in my husband's massive shoulders, thick legs, almost shoulder length hair and beard. He's looking at the TV so I can't see his deep-set eyes and the other side of his face, yet, I've memorized their light gray color and the pink, rough looking skin on the right side of his face. A shiver runs through me.

Ransom turns toward me. I look away. Heat creeps up my face when I'm caught staring. I look at the cracking logs in the log burner and the heat in my body intensifies. I bite my lip. For years I didn't feel any desire and thought part of me had dried up with the bitterness from my past life, but the moment I laid eyes on Ransom a few months ago, lust stirred in me.

“Do you want to watch something else?”

His voice is deep, steady and quiet, just like him. It makes me think of strength and loyalty. As if it’s the voice of someone I can trust. Which is bull considering his humongous size and bad boy look. Ransom Boyd is not the type of man a mother would look at and think of as a prospective husband for her daughter. That doesn’t faze me because one, I don’t have a mother or father, and two, I lived with the kind of white collar, handsome boy society believed made perfect husband material and went through hell.

“No, I like this.” And I do like the soap that’s playing. It’s just that there’s zero chance of me paying attention to it tonight. “I really don’t mind if you want to watch something else, too.” His profile from the matchmaking agency said he likes nature shows.

“Willow.”

Even though I’m already looking at him, something in his voice and face makes me more alert.

“Didn’t we decide we’d take turns choosing?” He asks.

I nod.

“It’ll be my turn tomorrow. If I change the channel, you’ll have two nights of watching animals in the wild. I won’t let go of the remote.”

His lip lifts a fraction. Is that an attempt at a joke?

My own lips tug up.

"I'll keep the drama on." I lift the remote off the coffee table and put it on the armrest on my side of the couch. Then I pick it up and press pause. "Ask away if there's anything you want explained." I've watched a third of the show but I started it at the beginning so he won't feel lost.

Ransom scratches his beard. "Why did Michael say he committed the crime when he clearly didn't?"

I can't help the smile that tugs at my lips. "You'll see."

Suddenly, some of the tension in me disappears. He's watching. It may seem like a small thing, but to me, it's a step in the right direction for this marriage that's based on the small amount of information we exchanged about each other on the matchmaking agency profile and the couple of times we met. He's trying to get along with me.

The first time I saw Ransom was three months ago, which was about nine months after I arrived in Blossom Ford on the run from my partner of four years. I was shocked by the lust he stirred in me, but I didn't approach him. I was too busy surviving. Stopping myself thinking about him at night became a problem I couldn't solve, so I stopped trying and when I felt horny, it was his eyes and body I saw when I made myself come.

Six weeks ago, my high school friend Coleen called and said my ex-partner was looking for me again. For days, I was paralyzed with fear. My ex-partner had found me before when I run to Chicago. I'd thought being in a large city would make it almost impossible for him to find me, but I was wrong and barely escaped. I ran as far south as I could go until my money run out in Blossom Ford.

I made a home for me and my little boy, Jordan. Jordan loves the friends he has made at Smart Teddies Day care, and I love my job there. I don't want to leave Blossom ford.

As I watched Jordan play on the swings at the park one Sunday, thinking about what to do, I sensed someone beside me. Terrified, I'd looked sideways to see Granny Tallulah sit on the other side of the bench I was sitting on. I'd seen her wandering about town when I first arrived in Blossom Ford a few weeks later I learned she had dementia so everyone in town looked out for her and walked her home if they found her out late at night or wandering the streets without shoes or a coat.

I think she thought I was her daughter because she always wanted to know what my little boy was eating and how he was doing and gave me advice to make him "big and strong" as she often said. That day, as I was leaving the park, Granny Tallulah grabbed my arm and said the strangest words. Her daughter would find me a husband who would protect me and my little boy. I remember the shiver that runs up my spine. Not even Angel knew about my past.

As I headed home, I told myself Granny Tallulah was probably speaking generally, but the thought that the agency had matched a lot of happy couples in Blossom Ford, including my newlywed friend Angel and her husband, kept intruding into my mind. I signed up and when I was matched with Ransom; I recognized him straight away. The fact he was ex-military and lived in the mountains grabbed my attention and wouldn't let go. I started wondering if maybe he could protect us. That it'd be harder to be found in the mountains.

His profile said he was looking for companionship and love. I should have skipped past his picture because I wasn't looking for love. My ex-partner was my high school sweetheart. When I fell for and started living with him, I thought I'd at last found true happiness. Instead, I'd swapped the hell of bad foster care and a rough group home for the hell of an abusive partner.

I hadn't planned to mention anything when I met Ransom. The fear he'd change his mind about our arranged marriage after learning about my past was absolute. However, despite his rough looks, or maybe because of it, I'd sensed an honesty in Ransom that made me ashamed of lying to him. Suddenly, hiding my past didn't feel right, and I told him I was running from my ex.

"I spent almost all of my adult life protecting people. It's the one thing I'm good at," he'd said in that steady voice of his and although a part of me was terrified of trusting a man with my life, I didn't have many other choices and went ahead with the marriage.

Seeing him try to keep to the small arrangement we made about taking turns doing what we each like together gives me some hope of us getting along.

MATCHED TO PATRICK

THE O'CONNORS OF BLOSSOM FORD #1

Patrick

MINGLED LAUGHTER DRIFTS from the sitting room, bringing mixed feelings of joy and sadness. We decorated the entire house in green–it's St Patrick's Day. As usual, we've been to church and are now having beef pot roast, which Mom and Aunt Shauna insist on making every year on the feast day of St. Patrick. Dad would have been so happy to hear that laughter. Even though we gathered like today at Christmas, St Patrick's Day was his favorite holiday.

I remove more salad from the refrigerator.

"Ready for the parade of women our moms no doubt have lined up for you this year?" My cousin Lorcan asks. I know his lilting voice like I know my own.

I snap the refrigerator closed. "Will I be the only one on display?"

He winces. "You're the eldest. And you're Aunt Caitlin's only son, so you'll definitely be in the firing line. Mom will surely want to marry Riordan off first. I'll be an afterthought."

The lump in my throat prevents me from chuckling. I can't really blame Lorcan. I used to be like him. The thought of marriage drove me barmy. Not anymore.

At first I couldn't imagine myself being happy with a family, not with the crushing guilt I felt over what happened to Little Fiona. Before Dad passed, he made me promise to let go of that guilt and cherish the time I've been blessed with. Although I believed it'd never happen, little by little, I'm appreciating life.

I want what Mom and Dad had, though. They were meant for each other. Someone out there is my soulmate and the moment I find her, I'm not letting go. For the last couple of years, Mom and Aunt Shauna's matchmaking efforts haven't bothered me in the least.

I glance outside to where Riordan, my cousin and Lorcan's eldest brother, sits in the spring sun. "Riordan is not ready to get married. I doubt he'll hang around for the picnic and anyone our moms might want to set him up with."

That giant of a man is still blaming himself for what happened to his little sister Fiona, even though it's been twenty-six years since she was taken from us. Our dads were first cousins -both O'Connors. The two of us are forty-four, but I'm older than Riordan by one week. As the oldest children in the O'Connor family, it was our responsibility to make sure Fiona was safe.

Lorcan opens the back door.

"Mom is calling," he says to Rio.

It's the only thing that'll move my eldest cousin. Aunt Shauna may not be calling him now, but Riordan knows she'll soon be, wanting to make sure he spends as much time with us as possible before he scoots up the mountain.

Riordan and Lorcan's six brothers and Dad are watching TV while Mom and Aunt Shauna are chat.

"Don't forget to take good care of my friend Nara when she gets here. She was very kind to me the other day in town when I forgot my wallet," Mom reminds me.

We spend another couple of hours leisurely drinking and chatting, then get up to prepare for the outdoor picnic, which starts at four. The whole town is invited to our farm. Our parents started the tradition a few years after settling in Blossom Ford and starting a lettuce farm together, because they missed spending St Patrick's Day with their large family back in Ireland.

We put up tents on the large grass area between my house and Riordan's. Mom and Aunt Shauna used to do all the food when they were younger, but now, Lorcan gets caterers in to bring sandwiches and other finger food. By the time the townsfolk arrive, Cormac and Emmet, my youngest cousins, have set up a DJ stand which is playing upbeat music and the entire field is filled with green bunting and balloons.

I'm taking a breather from greeting people when I see a woman strolling towards Mom. Something about the way she walks catches my attention. She's wearing black skinny jeans that mold her curvy ass to perfection and a light green top that covers a pair of generous breasts and complements the sun-kissed tone of her skin. Wavy jet-black hair falls below her shoulders and shimmers in the sun.

I'm too far away to see the color of her eyes. Before I know it, I'm marching towards Mom, curiosity and something I can't name, compelling me forward.

"I'm so glad you came, Nara," Mom is saying when I reach her side on a strategic part of the field where she, Aunt Shauna, and their friend Ms. Penny can see everyone.

Tawny, that's the color of her eyes.

I answer myself as Nara greets everyone with an amiable smile that reaches her almond-shaped, yellow-brown eyes and warms the inside of my chest. She's comfortable around Mom, Aunt Shauna and their friends, even though she must be in her mid-twenties. The silver hoops on the tops of her ears glint in the sunshine.

"This is my son, Patrick." Mom points to me.

I stretch out my hand in greeting and when she holds mine; hers is small and smooth against my large and calloused one. I don't let go and she glances up at me.

That's when I know. That I've found the woman I've spent the last few years searching for.

The friendly warmth on her face is replaced by something else: interest. A tinge of pink fills her cheeks before she pulls her hand away.

Her voice cracks a little when she says hello leaving me to wonder where the confidence she exhibited a few moments ago went.

"I'll show you where the food is," I say.

"I don't want to trouble you." She looks about her. "I'll find it, thank you."

"It's no trouble at all," Mom beams at Nara. "Patrick will walk you over to the food area. Just ask him if there's anything you need to know."

A frown forms on my face as I lead the way. At my age, I'm old enough to know when a woman has the hots for me. I know Nara fancies me, but she's decided not to pursue it.

If there's one thing I'm good at, is getting to the root of a problem. Now I've found Nara, I'll have to convince her I'm the only man for her.

OTHER BOOKS BY THE AUTHOR

CURVY BRIDES OF BLOSSOM FORD SERIES

MARRYING THE PROTECTIVE PROFESSOR

MARRYING THE GRUMPY DIRECTOR

MARRYING THE POSSESSIVE NEIGHBOR

MARRYING THE WIDOWED DOCTOR

MARRYING THE SCARRED SOLDIER

MARRYING THE OBSESSIVE CEO

MARRYING THE BIG MOUNTAIN MAN

THE O'CONNORS OF BLOSSOM FORD SERIES

MATCHED TO PATRICK

ABOUT THE AUTHOR

Iris West writes short and spicy romance about alpha heroes and the women they can't help falling in love with. She loves reading all types of romance books that have a happy ending and is an avid Kdrama fan.

Follow or like her on Facebook and Goodreads.

FREE BOOK

Would you like a free book? Sign up to my mailing list at https://dl.bookfunnel.com/t191w45ryj to receive a copy of Loving My Fake Husband, a free to subscribers only, Curvy Brides of Blossom Ford Series short story.

HELP OTHERS FIND THIS BOOK

Thank you for reading Marrying The Widowed Doctor. If you enjoyed this book, please help others discover it by leaving a review at your favorite online book store.

Many thanks,

Iris xx

www.ingramcontent.com/pod-product-compliance
Ingram Content Group UK Ltd.
Pitfield, Milton Keynes, MK11 3LW, UK
UKHW042000190726
13854UKWH00005B/2078

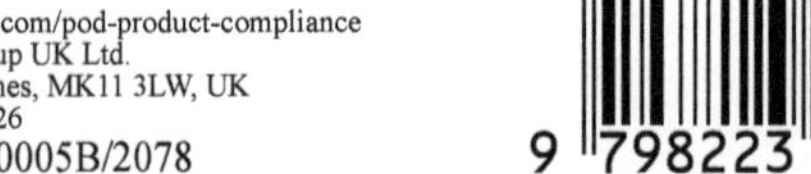

9 798223 704232